WHITE RAINBOW,
BLACK CURSE

BOOK 1 IN THE
KANA'IAUPUNI SERIES

WHITE RAINBOW, BLACK CURSE

THE STORY OF
KAMEHAMEHA'S BIRTH

DAVID KĀWIKA EYRE

ILLUSTRATED BY
IMAIKALANI KALAHELE

KAMEHAMEHA PUBLISHING

HONOLULU

The Kanaʻiaupuni Series is a work of historic fiction about Kamehameha, the great hero of Hawaiʻi. The series highlights the people, places, and events that shaped Kamehameha's life and led him to become the Conqueror of the Islands. The stories are based on Hawaiian sources and are intended for students, families, and educators.

Note: The title *White Rainbow, Black Curse* reflects a Hawaiian association of death with the color black. Black also holds positive connotations, as with a puaʻa hiwa or black pig reserved as an offering in heiau ceremonies.

KAMEHAMEHA SCHOOLS

Copyright © 2007 by David L. Eyre

Inquiries should be addressed to:
Kamehameha Publishing
567 S. King Street
Honolulu, Hawaiʻi 96813

ISBN 978-0-87336-117-0

Design by Viki Nasu Design Group

Printed in China

12 11 10 09 08 07   5 4 3 2 1

He Ho‘omana‘o iā Pauahi
Dedicated to Pauahi

They pointed to the star and exclaimed: "A white rainbow!"
It was the unmistakable sign of a great chief's birth.

I t was a time of many prayers, some of life, some of death. Kokoiki at Kohala was the place, and the month was 'Ikuwā. Men's thoughts were of war and sea and storm and an astonishing star seen streaming across the northern sky. They pointed to the star and exclaimed: "A white rainbow!" It was the unmistakable sign of a great chief's birth.

The sky was cut by jagged lightning, a sky both bright and dark. Where the land sloped low to the coast, the flash of white lightning showed in blurry outline an encampment of warriors and long lines of beached canoes. It was a fleet made ready for revenge. Alapaʻinui, the high chief of Hawaiʻi, sought vengeance on Maui chief Kekaulike for his recent raids on Kona and Kohala. Gathered that night on the stormy shores of Kohala were ten thousand warriors and their aliʻi, among them Alapaʻinui, Keawemaʻuhili, Kalaniʻōpuʻu, Keaweokahikona, Keōuakupua, and Kekūhaupiʻo.

And at Kokoiki that night as well, in the rounded body of his mother Kekuʻiapoiwa, was the unborn chief Kamehameha, he who one day would be the greatest aliʻi of all.

Nearby, winds hushed a whispered chant that cursed this child soon to be born. It was a chant to choke.

Hunched over in his shadowed hut, bent like a dog's back leg, a kahuna squeezed his eyes and s queezed his fists as he uttered his curse repeatedly, each time drawing on a single breath:

> "Faint, be faint, faint, faint.
> He gasps, gasps.
> Now pinch him, strangle him,
> Pinch his eyes to blind him.
> His nose, pinch it too.
> His mouth, pinch it, close it.
> His windpipe, seize, choke, strangle!"

The kahuna blinked his blurry eyes and ended his curse with these words: "Die! You will die! I send you death!" He ate a small worm to hasten the curse along, and grew quiet.

Nearby, winds hushed a whispered chant
that cursed this child soon to be born.

On the beach, through a driven rain of many droplets, a birth kahuna just as determinedly chanted for the life of the unborn child. "Live! You will live! Death returns to its sender!"

The wind whipped her wet hair as her hands carried the young leaves of the pōhuehue, handed to her by a runner from the beach at Lapakahi. The leaves gleamed in the wet dark when the lightning flashed on them. Holding up five leaves in her right hand, she prayed to Kū. Holding up five leaves in her left hand, she prayed to Hina.

Then, leaves in hand, the kahuna returned to the house where Kekuʻiapoiwa, the rounded mother, prepared for the birth. Two sullen guards were posted in front. They had orders from Alapaʻinui to seize the child at his first cry and to kill him. But the guards slumped, heavy-lidded and cold, their heads drooped down despite the slashing lightning. The kahuna was careful to make no sound.

Two sullen guards … had orders
to seize the child at his first cry and to kill him.

Inside, the kahuna gave the leaves in her right hand to
Keku'iapoiwa to eat, for they would hasten the birth. She took
a small stone mortar and ground the rest of the leaves to rub
over the rounded 'ōpū. The pain of birth burned in there like
an imu stone.

In the shadows behind the thatched house a dark, kneeling figure
was also preparing for the birth. It was Nae'ole, a young chief
of Kohala, a man loyal to this mother and her unborn child. His
fingers worked quickly to loosen several sheaves of pili thatch
that ran the length of the wall. When the time came, he would
shove the thatch to the side and open a space big enough for the
kahuna to pass the baby through.

Keku'iapoiwa squatted on layers of soft matting. In the light of a kukui lamp, her belly gleamed like a gourd. The look in her eyes was both inward and outward. Like the drumming thunder, the pain within came and went, came and went. Outside, glancing from the corners of his eyes, Nae'ole listened for the baby to be born.

In the months before, the birth kahuna had prepared her high chiefess for this child. As Keku'iapoiwa's body slowly swelled, the kahuna rubbed kukui oil on her. At the beach she showed Keku'iapoiwa how to move her 'ōpū gently from side to side in the warm water. This would loosen the baby.

Keku'iapoiwa ate the orange 'ilima blossoms and the thick end of the yellow-petaled hau flowers brought by her kahuna. These also would help the baby slip out more easily.

But as Keku'iapoiwa's body grew bulky with baby, it was not the delicate 'ilima blossom that she yearned to eat. She craved instead the eye of the frightful niuhi shark, the chief of the deep ocean. This was a sign that the child was a boy, that he would be fierce, and grow up to be a slayer of chiefs.

Alapa'inui, the ali'i of Hawai'i, knew this, for there were many stories of the niuhi shark that thrashed through the water, grabbed a man, and shook him up and down in the sea. This boy child must be killed before he could kill and conquer others.

Curiously, however, as the threats to the unborn child continued, the usual preparations for the birth of a high chief began, as if this child were to live. Chanters in the court composed chants, and dancers practiced new hula to celebrate his genealogy.

But the council of chiefs did not forget that the mother of this child craved the eye of the niuhi shark, and Keawema'uhili, the chief of Hilo, insisted that the child must die. "Pinch off the tip of the young wauke shoot," he whispered to Alapa'inui in a voice of stone.

She craved the eye of the frightful niuhi shark,
the chief of the deep ocean.

And so it was that the guards were ordered to stand watch at the hale. As the rain roared like the ocean, the guards listened for the baby they would smother as soon as he breathed.

But Kekuʻiapoiwa had other plans for her son. She squatted on the layered mats, facing the birth kahuna. She put her arms around the kahuna's neck, and the kahuna spoke to her, soothed her, encouraged her. "'Ume i ka hanu!" were her words as the pain tightened. "Draw the breath! Draw the breath!" Their voices were hushed so as not to attract the attention of the guards. "E hoʻomanawanui! Be patient! It will not be long now."

Then, in the yellow glow of the ihoiho kukui, the firm hands of the kahuna pressed down on the rounded ʻōpū of Kekuʻiapoiwa. Her whispered words pressed down as well: "Push! Push now! Push hard!" The pain peaked and the head could be seen. The kahuna worked the little body along the narrow place. At last she exclaimed in a hushed voice, a voice lower than the rush of the rain on the thatch: "'Ike ʻia nā maka i ke ao! The eyes are seen in the world! The child is born!"

She laid the wet baby on white kapa, a kapa lighter than moon-
light and warmed by warm pebbles. She pulled the soft cloth
around him and began to chant. Her voice was quiet and steady
and glowing like kukui light. The sound shone on the child. It
was a chant nearly wordless, a murmur more of her mind than
her mouth. She chanted the child's genealogy. She called upon
his kūpuna to protect him in the days to come. She chanted to
give new life to the words of Kapoukahi from Kauaʻi who had
prophesied this child's great deeds. Then the kahuna took a
short, sharp piece of bamboo and cut the piko. Still chanting,
she wiped the baby clean.

All the while, the mother Kekuʻiapoiwa watched, listened and
joined in the chant. As she chanted, she fixed her strong gaze in
the eyes of the baby. The baby stared back at her face in silence.
The gentle mana of the mother held him and he did not cry out.

The kahuna dipped her fingers into warm kamani oil, slipped
her hands beneath the kapa and rubbed the oil on the newborn's
body. Then she wrapped him in kapa and handed the bundle to

Keku'iapoiwa who lay on the matting. There was little time. Nae'ole crouched outside the thick pili wall, glancing from the corners of his eyes.

Keku'iapoiwa pressed her nose into the baby's neck. Her eyes closed and she breathed in deeply. The baby smelled of warm kamani oil. Then, without a word, the kahuna took the bundle and passed it through the opening to Nae'ole.

His back to the rain, Nae'ole pulled the kapa around the head of the child, clasped the bundle against his chest, and vanished into the morning darkness.

Lightning crackled across the blackened sky. Nae'ole ran with the bundle along the coast downslope of where the many warriors were camped. The way was dark and blurred by rain, but this was his land, and his feet knew the path like eyes.

This was his land, and his feet knew the path like eyes.

Daylight came slowly in grays. The guards pushed their way into the birthing hale but found only a sleeping mother with no child. Their eyes widened; their mouths opened, wordless. When the guards told Alapaʻinui of the baby's disappearance, he ordered them to search throughout Kohala—and dare not return until the child was found and destroyed. In Kohala that day, they set torch to thatch, they ransacked and burned.

Naeʻole ran past the thick gray walls of Moʻokini heiau. Inside the hale mana, the dog-toothed grimace of the war god Kūkāʻilimoku gleamed in the dark. Beneath blunt black eyebrows, the white pearl shell of his eyes stirred.

Naeʻole stopped, looked around, and stepped close. He pulled back the kapa from the baby's face. Naeʻole's breath broke the stillness. He whispered:

"E kuʻu keiki aloha, here is our god." Naeʻole's chest heaved. "See the mouth. See the eyes. They too are of rainbow! In your life, his eyes and his mouth will be for you. This too, my beloved child, is your destiny!"

Naeʻole knew he was being pursued. He ran past one group of houses and on to the next. People who had prayed for the baby's birth awaited his passing. They looked at the bundle with eyes that knew. Women nursed the child. They gave Naeʻole food and small gourds of water. Then they hid in their hale. Naeʻole ran on in the rain.

It was days later when Naeʻole finally reached the place called ʻĀwini, high in the hills of Kohala. His breath burned. The wind had quieted, and a mist was lifting from the drenched hills. In the slanting light, a rainbow curved over a cave, a sign that the land awaited its chief.

Inside the cave a woman also waited. Her name was Kaha. She sat on a mat on the cool floor nursing her own child, a girl named Kuakāne. When Naeʻole entered, Kaha put her child down on the mat beside her.

"Here!" she smiled to Naeʻole, holding out her hands for the bundle, "Give me the little lonely one, this little Kamehameha!"

She pulled the baby to her breast, naming him as she did. And so it was that he was called Kamehameha, "the lonely one."

"Quick! Hide him! There is little time!" Naeʻole blurted, his eyes darkening, "They will soon be here!"

Kaha's mother Hiku followed Naeʻole as he rushed outside. She made her way to where the sheer cliff dropped deep into the valley.

She could hear voices coming closer, harsh words thrusting through the mossy ʻōhiʻa lehua branches along the rim of the pali.

Naeʻole disappeared into the forest behind her as she whispered a chant to Kāne, god of waters, maker of thunder:

"E Kāne ē, take the rising red rain, take the rainbow that curves over the cave. Return, return them to the mother at Kokoiki. They will only guide the executioners and their killing thoughts to this hiding place of our royal child."

She could hear voices coming closer, harsh words thrusting
through the mossy ʻōhiʻa lehua branches along the rim of the pali.

The mists rose and the rainbow faded. But the harsh words grew louder through the 'ōhi'a trees.

Hiku rushed into the cave where the baby Kamehameha, now warm and fed, had dozed off. She glanced about the kukui-lit cave. In a corner, behind coils of hala leaves, was a large basket filled with olonā fiber. She lifted the tangled fiber from the basket and carefully laid the sleeping Kamehameha inside. Then she spread the fiber over him without waking him.

Moments later, the executioners burst into the cave, their faces fierce and dirty, their arms glistening with sweat. Short black spears jerked in their fists as they spoke: "Have you seen a runner pass this way?" Not waiting for an answer, they lit two kukui torches and began searching the cave. Flickering flames cast smoke in the air. Jagged shadows cut across the floor. They searched to where the ceiling slanted to the ground and where dried fish and salt were stored in small baskets, but they did not bother with the basket of olonā fiber. Kuakāne, the girl child, began to cry. Kaha picked her up to nurse her, praying that Kamehameha in the basket would not awaken.

Then, as abruptly as they arrived, the executioners rushed off, never to return. The royal child was spared.

The executioners burst into the cave, their faces fierce and dirty,
their arms glistening with sweat.

Kamehameha, the boy who would one day be called Kanaʻiaupuni, the Conqueror of the Islands, spent many months in the cave at ʻĀwini, high in the hills of Kohala. It was a thickly forested place facing the dark ocean. Kaha cared for both children. At night, after nursing, she laid them on the kapa and sang them to sleep, repeating the same soft words over and over:

"The birds are going to sleep … The flowers are going to sleep … The fish are ready to sleep …"

As Kamehameha grew, Kaha and her mother Hiku gave him sweetened poi sucked off the tip of the small finger, and sweet potatoes, chewed by one of the women and passed from her mouth to his mouth. Naeʻole went down to the sea, bringing back ʻopihi and ʻaʻama crabs to make broth for the boy. From early on, the children were fed mashed sweet potato leaves, sweetened with the juice of toasted sugarcane and the droplets of honey that formed at the tip of banana blossoms.

Night after night, when eating was done and eyelids were heavy, the sleep song began again: "The birds are going to sleep … The flowers are going to sleep … The fish are ready to sleep …"

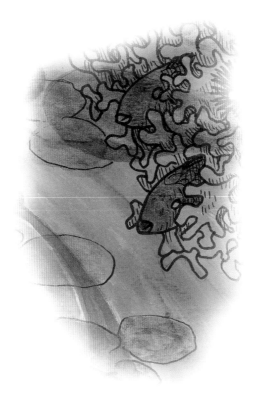

"The birds are going to sleep … The flowers are going to sleep …
The fish are ready to sleep …"

Well into the days when Kamehameha was walking, Kaha and Hiku decided the time had come to wean him. By now the family had moved from the cave at ʻĀwini down to the valley of Hālawa where they lived near the stream, inland from the shore.

One morning, Kaha sat in front of a small calabash of water. Kamehameha sat in the curve of her arm. Facing them, Hiku began her chanting. "E Kū! E Hina! Eia ke keiki! Here is the child …" She chanted firmly, leaned forward, and floated two white flowers in the calabash. Kamehameha saw the flowers. He grasped for them with his little hands and flung them impatiently to the side, indicating by an ancient ritual that he was ready to stop drinking milk. Hiku then asked, "Kamehameha, do you wish the desire for milk to go away?" Speaking for Kamehameha, Kaha answered, "ʻAe. Yes." "And never more will you desire milk?" Kaha smiled at the child and again answered for him: "ʻAʻole loa! Never!"

That evening a feast was held to mark the end of Kamehameha's nursing. The feast lasted late into the night, and lids were heavy. A sleeping puppy pushed its paws against a calabash, and Kamehameha snuggled down in his kapa, a kapa white as moon-light. The boy who would one day become the fierce niuhi shark of the battlefields, the great Kanaʻiaupuni, yawned. And his lashes lay down on his cheeks.

"The birds are going to sleep … The flowers are going to sleep …
The fish are ready to sleep … The birds are going to sleep …
The flowers are going to sleep … The fish are ready to sleep …"

The stars were high. The moon was low, and a woman's voice
trailed out into the soft night.

MAHALO

 am indebted to the many kumu—sources or teachers—whose work is the foundation for all we do. The works of Mary Kawena Pukui are a major source for this story, including the curse, the "sleeping song," and information about traditional birthing and weaning practices. I have borrowed from Mrs. Pukui with the greatest respect and gratitude.

Kēhau Cachola-Abad has prodded the text in important ways—especially given her family roots that trace deep into Kohala. Gavan Daws has been supportive of this project and has my sincere gratitude and aloha for his many contributions. Imaikalani Kalahele has produced images of extraordinary power, cultural complexity, and beauty. Keʻala Kwan's instinctive cultural insight has helped to focus these stories. Clemi McLaren has been encouraging and generous in every way. Sigrid Southworth has provided constructive criticism and a keen sense of this land. Anna Sumida contributed enthusiasm and an experienced eye for young readers. Henry Bennett and Waimea Williams have been wonderful in guiding this work toward publication.

Others who have supported this project include Sally and Chris Aall, Julian Ako, Elizabeth Boynton, Fred Cachola, Megan Clark, Bernard Corbe, Matthew Corry, Kelsi Cottrell, Conard Eyre, David W. Eyre, Gail Fujimoto, Dani Gardner, Kaiponohea Hale, Herb Kāne, Kawika Makanani, Tyna Millacci, Terina Morris, Saul Nakayama, Bonnie Ozaki-James, William Kalikolehua Pānui, Mike Racoma, Kim and Jim Slagel, Kalani Soller, Kaleo Trinidad, Keola and Ipo Wong, Mimi Wong, and my children: Sintra, Lisa, Emma, Makana and Alea.

Many students at Kamehameha Schools have provided invaluable assistance and insight. I thank Kanoa Cleveland, Kela Nakama, Mackensie Friel, Robert Landgraf, Kani Keahi, Kepola Iervolino, Hiʻilaniwai Kaneʻe, Sanoe Keliʻinoi, Kamakana Kinzie, Kaui Kuaiwa, Hoʻomaluhia Lee, Nahenahe McMillan, Puaʻalaikahonihoʻomau Pascua, Kaʻawaloa Sam, Pomaikaʻiokalani Wai, and the fourth grade students of teachers Jan Furuta, Michelle Anguay-Sagon, and Winona Farias.

I am grateful to Nā Kumu o Kamehameha, Kaʻiwakīloumoku, Hoʻokahua, and Kamehameha Publishing for their inspiration and support. The mistakes that remain are mine alone. Mahalo nui iā ʻoukou pākahi a pau.

D.K.E.
March 2007

GLOSSARY

GODS & PEOPLE

Alapaʻinui · high chief of Hawaiʻi Island at Kamehameha's birth

Hiku · mother of Kaha, "step-grandmother" of Kamehameha at birth

Hina · a widely known goddess associated with healing; wife of Kū

Kaha · "stepmother" of Kamehameha at his birth

Kalaniʻōpuʻu · high chief of Hawaiʻi Island as Kamehameha reached adulthood

Kamehameha · the great hero of Hawaiʻi 1758(?) – 1819

Kanaʻiaupuni · the Conqueror of the Islands

Kāne · one of four main Hawaiian gods

Kapoukahi · Kauaʻi priest who prophesied Kamehameha's greatness

Keawemaʻuhili · high chief of Hilo, Hawaiʻi

Keaweokahikona · son of Keawemaʻuhili and Ululani

Kekaulike · chief of Maui at time of Kamehameha's birth

Kekūhaupiʻo · aliʻi, famous warrior, became Kamehameha's teacher and advisor

Kekuʻiapoiwa · mother of Kamehameha

Keōuakupua · father of Kamehameha

Kuakāne · young daughter of Kaha, older "stepsister" of Kamehameha

Kū (Kūkāʻilimoku) · one of the four main Hawaiian gods; in this form, god of war

Naeʻole · chief of Kohala who saved Kamehameha's life after his birth

PLACES

ʻĀwini · land section in North Kohala

Hālawa · valley of Kamehameha's childhood in North Kohala

Hawaiʻi · largest of Hawaiian Islands

Hilo · district and bay on eastern Hawaiʻi Island

Kauaʻi · oldest island in Hawaiian group, northeast of Oʻahu

Kohala · district in northwest Hawaiʻi Island

Kokoiki · birthplace of Kamehameha, located in Kohala

Kona · leeward district on Hawaiʻi Island

Lapakahi · beach and land section in North Kohala

Maui · second largest island in the Hawaiian group

Moʻokini · heiau in Kohala district near Kamehameha's birthplace

OTHER HAWAIIAN WORDS

'a'ama · black crab that lives on shore rocks
'Ae · Yes
ali'i · chief, ruler
'A'ole loa · Never
E ho'omanawanui · Be patient
E ku'u keiki aloha · My beloved child
Eia ke keiki · Here is the child
hala · pandanus tree
hale · house
hale mana · most sacred hale in a heiau used by a ruling chief
hau · lowland tree of the hibiscus family
heiau · Hawaiian place of worship
hula · traditional Hawaiian form of dance
ihoiho kukui · kukui nut candle
'Ike 'ia nā maka i ke ao · The eyes are seen in the world
'Ikuwā · stormy month of the year (October/November)
'ilima · native shrub with orange-yellow flowers
imu · underground oven
kahuna (pl. kāhuna) · priest, sorcerer, expert in any profession
kamani · a large tree, common near shore, its nut
kapa · tapa, a cloth made from bark
kukui · candlenut tree, the nut of this tree
kupuna (pl. kūpuna) · grandparent, ancestor
mana · supernatural or divine power; spiritual or personal force
niuhi · large, man-eating shark
'ōhi'a lehua · common tree producing wood and flowers
olonā · native shrub; inner bark used to make strong cordage
'opihi · limpet
'ōpū · stomach
pali · cliff
piko · umbilical cord
pili · grass used for thatching Hawaiian houses
pōhuehue · beach morning-glory
poi · food staple from pounded taro corms
'Ume i ka hanu · Draw the breath
wauke · a tree whose inner bark was used for making cloth

The Hawaiian words in this text have been recorded to make correct pronunciation available to readers and students. Warmest mahalo to Hawaiian language teachers Māhealani Chang and Ke'ala Kwan for recording these words. To hear the words, go to http://publishing.ksbe.edu/ and click on the book title link.

SELECTED BIBLIOGRAPHY

The sources listed below form the kahua or foundation of *White Rainbow, Black Curse*. Though not an exhaustive list, the selected bibliography indicates the key sources consulted for this story and provides a starting point for further research on the life of Kamehameha.

Beckwith, Martha Warren. *Kepelino's Traditions of Hawai'i*. Bernice P. Bishop Museum Bulletin 95. Honolulu: Bishop Museum Press, 1932.

Buck, Peter H. [Te Rangi Hiroa]. *Arts and Crafts of Hawai'i*. Honolulu: Bishop Museum Press, 1957.

Daws, Gavan. *Shoal of Time: A History of the Hawaiian Islands*. Toronto: MacMillan, 1968.

Desha, Stephen Langhern. *Kamehameha and His Warrior Kekūhaupi'o*. Translated by Frances N. Frazier. Honolulu: Kamehameha Schools Press, 2000.

Elbert, Samuel H., Esther T. Mookini, and Mary Kawena Pukui. *Place Names of Hawai'i*. 2nd ed. Honolulu: University of Hawai'i Press, 1974.

Handy, Edward Smith Craighill, and Elizabeth Green Handy. With Mary Kawena Pukui. *Native Planters in Old Hawai'i: Their Life, Lore, and Environment*. Bernice P. Bishop Museum Bulletin 233. Honolulu: Bishop Museum Press, 1972.

Handy, Edward Smith Craighill, and Mary Kawena Pukui. *The Polynesian Family System in Ka'ū, Hawai'i*. Rutland, VT: Charles E. Tuttle, 1972.

Ii, John Papa. *Fragments of Hawaiian History*. Edited by Dorothy Benton Barrère. Translated by Mary Kawena Pukui. Honolulu: Bishop Museum Press, 1959.

Judd, Walter F. *Kamehameha*. Edited by Robert B. Goodman and Robert A. Spicer. Hong Kong: Mandarin Ltd., 1976.

Kalākaua, David. *Legends and Myths of Hawai'i*. Rutland, VT: Charles E. Tuttle, 1972.

Kamakau, Samuel Mānaiakalani. *Ruling Chiefs of Hawai'i*. Honolulu: Kamehameha Schools Press, 1961.

Kamakau, Samuel Mānaiakalani. *Ka Poʻe Kahiko: The People of Old.* Edited by Dorothy Benton Barrère. Translated by Mary Kawena Pukui. Honolulu: Bishop Museum Press, 1964.

———. *Tales and Traditions of the People of Old: Nā Moʻolelo a ka Poʻe Kahiko.* Honolulu: Bishop Museum Press, 1991.

———. *The Works of the People of Old: Nā Hana a ka Poʻe Kahiko.* Honolulu: Bishop Museum Press, 1976.

Kanahele, George Heʻeu Sanford. *Kū Kanaka, Stand Tall: A Search for Hawaiian Values.* Honolulu: University of Hawaiʻi Press, 1986.

Kāne, Herb Kawainui. *Ancient Hawaiʻi.* Captain Cook, HI: Kawainui Press, 1997.

———. *Voyagers.* Edited by Paul Berry. Bellevue, WA: WhaleSong, 1991.

Kōmike Huaʻōlelo, Hale Kuamoʻo, ʻAha Pūnana Leo. *Māmaka Kaiao: A Modern Hawaiian Vocabulary.* Honolulu: University of Hawaiʻi Press, 1998.

Kuykendall, Ralph S. *The Hawaiian Kingdom.* Vol. 1, *1778–1854, Foundation and Transformation.* University of Hawaiʻi Press, 1938.

Malo, David. *Hawaiian Antiquities.* 2nd ed. Translated by Nathaniel B. Emerson. Bernice P. Bishop Museum Special Publication 2. Honolulu: Bishop Museum Press, 1951.

McKinzie, Edith Kawelo Kapule. "An Original Narrative of Kamehameha the Great, Written in *Ka Naʻi Aupuni* (1905–1906) by Joseph M. Poepoe." Master's thesis, University of Hawaiʻi–Mānoa, 1982.

Mellen, Kathleen Dickenson. *The Lonely Warrior.* New York: Hastings House, 1949.

Pukui, Mary Kawena. *ʻŌlelo Noʻeau: Hawaiian Proverbs and Poetical Sayings.* Bernice P. Bishop Museum Special Publication 71. Honolulu: Bishop Museum Press, 1983.

Pukui, Mary Kawena, and Samuel H. Elbert. *Hawaiian Dictionary.* 2nd ed. Honolulu: University of Hawaiʻi Press, 1986.

Pukui, Mary Kawena, E. W. Haertig, and Catherine A. Lee. *Nānā i Ke Kumu: Look to the Source.* 2 vols. Honolulu: Queen Liliʻuokalani Children's Center–Hui Hānai, 1979.

Tregaskis, Richard. *The Warrior King.* New York: MacMillan, 1973.

KAMEHAMEHA PUBLISHING

Kamehameha Publishing supports Kamehameha Schools' mission by publishing and distributing Hawaiian language, culture, and community-based materials that engage, reinforce, and invigorate Hawaiian cultural vitality.

Our efforts are aligned with Kamehameha Schools' Strategic Plan 2000–2015. Kamehameha Publishing also advances the Education Strategic Plan approved in 2005, which seeks to create long-term intergenerational change. Kamehameha Publishing's materials address the needs of children, parents/caregivers, educators, and communities—the four core groups identified by the Education Strategic Plan.

Kamehameha Schools was founded in 1887 by the Last Will and Testament of Princess Bernice Pauahi Bishop, the great-granddaughter of Kamehameha I. At the time of Pauahi's death, the Hawaiian population had plummeted catastrophically due to diseases introduced by foreign contact. A century after Captain James Cook arrived in Hawai'i in 1778, the Hawaiian population had dwindled from an estimated 800,000 to 47,000.

At a time of great change, Princess Pauahi anticipated that education would strengthen and sustain her people. She left nearly her entire estate—375,000 acres of land—for the foundation and perpetual operation of the Kamehameha Schools for Boys and Girls. Today, roughly 700 students a year graduate from Kamehameha Schools' three K–12 campuses on O'ahu, Maui, and Hawai'i. Kamehameha Schools operates several preschools, provides preschool and postgraduate scholarships, and offers enrichment and literacy programs, giving preference to students of Hawaiian ancestry. It also provides funding for Hawaiian-focused and conversion public charter schools in predominantly Hawaiian communities.

▼▲▼▲▼▲▼▲▼▲▼▲▼▲▼▲▼▲▼▲▼▲▼▲▼▲▼▲▼▲▼▲▼▲▼

FIVE TIPS
FOR APPLYING THE LESSONS OF THIS BOOK

1. **'Ōpio** (children and youth)
   White Rainbow, Black Curse describes the birth of Kamehameha and how he was named. Talk with your mākua (parents) and kūpuna (grandparents) about your own birth and how they chose your inoa (name). Ask them about other interesting birth stories in your 'ohana and about other family names.

2. **'Ohana** (extended family)
   The story of Kamehameha's birth reflects the history of an 'ohana and its strong connections to the place and people of Kohala. Gather your own family stories and share reflections about your 'ohana's relationship to different places. Find creative ways to record these stories using photos, drawings, narratives, videos, and DVDs.

3. **Papa kula** (classroom)
   - Include the Hawaiian vocabulary in *White Rainbow, Black Curse* in everyday classroom discussions. Visit http://publishing.ksbe.edu to hear the correct pronunciation of Hawaiian words used in this story.
   - A lot of interesting things happened before, during, and after Kamehameha's birth. To illustrate the cause-and-effect relationships in these stories, have students work in groups to retell the events through skits, mural drawings, or other creative projects.
   - Kamehameha's first days illustrate how a single individual can affect the outcome of major historical events. Nae'ole's difficult journey to 'Āwini and Kaha's daily nurturing of the infant Kamehameha were important acts in the larger storyline of Kamehameha uniting the Hawaiian Islands. Help students imagine what roles they play—and will play—in shaping the history of their family, community, and lāhui.

4. **Kaiaulu** (community)
   In the story, the people of Kohala came together to protect the newborn Kamehameha and mālama (to care for) him in his early years. Think of the many things your community does—and needs to do more of—to work together in caring for one another and the 'āina that sustains the community.

5. **Lāhui** (people, nation)
   Kamehameha's story is ultimately about the unification of a people. What lessons can be applied from this history toward the goal of strengthening Hawaiians' shared cultural, social, and political identity?

FIND OUT MORE ...

How does Kamehameha overcome challenges and fulfill his chiefly destiny?

What trials and dangers await him?

What forces propel Kamehameha to become Kana'iaupuni, the Conquer of the Islands?

Read additional books in the **Kana'iaupuni Series** to find out!